NAH ME!

written by
Samantha V. Williams

Illustrated by
Taranggana

"Nah-Me"

by Samantha V. Williams

Illustrated by Taranggana

A percentage of the proceeds of this book will go towards charitable organisations in St. Vincent and the Grenadines that are commissioned to support boys and girls in their development.

"Nah Me" is a mysterious being who lives in every Caribbean house. Often unseen it is impossible to identify who he or she may be. Adults for years have explored every nook and cranny of their homes, still unable to tell how "Nah Me" looks. They cannot tell if "Nah Me" is as big as a house, as small as a mouse, short, tall, fat or thin. All they know is that she or he is the one blamed for every mischief made.

The Lonnisons were a family of seven;
Lorna the mom, Leonard the dad, Lea the oldest at 10 years old, Lucas was 9, Lily 7, Levi 5, and Leo the youngest of the bunch was 3 years old.

As you would imagine in a house with this many children there was always something mischievous happening which kept Mom on her toes.

Mom encouraged play, she thought it was a fun way for the children to learn so she was never too troubled about a little mess here and there.

However, when she asked any of her children who did something that they probably should not have done she always heard, it's "Nah Me".

On one particular day, Mom was overwhelmed with the number of mischievous incidents and the mess made. She gathered all five of her children and sat them down, determined to identify who exactly this "Nah Me" is, today.

"Children, can someone tell me who ate all
of the cookies from the cookie jar?" Mom asked,
Everyone chorused as if their response
was planned, "Nah Me."

Dissatisfied with their response,
Mom continued,
"Okay, who broke the new remote
control car?"
"Nah Me" they all said again.

"Tell me this," Mom questioned,
"who spilled grape juice on the living
room rug?"
The children sat quietly, with their
shoulders shrugged.

Unwavering, Mom asked,

"Who had the bright idea to paint the dog?

Come on, come on," she asked now

starting to shout.

"Someone talk! "Polka-dotted pink and

brown, who painted the dog?"

"Nah-Me," the children continued to exclaim;

but each time they said it their faces hung

in shame.

Mom decided to try a different approach,

offering them a reward in exchange for

the truth she thought maybe more successful.

"Okay, kids,"

She said,

"Whoever speaks the truth gets the best and

biggest ice cream sundae ever made!"

and again she asked,

"Who took a chunk out of the chocolate cake

that I made for the school's bake sale and left

a huge mess on the couch?"

Before the children could respond mom

continued again,

"Which of you tracked mud all through the house?"

"Nah Me!" the children disappointingly said.

By now you can hear a pin drop in the house,

but Mom needed to know,

 "Who dug up the roses in my flower bed?"

'Who knocked over the tools in Dad's tool shed?'

"Wait don't say a word let me guess, "Nah Me!"

Mom said, very certain of what their answer will be.

"Tell me kids," she continued,

"Help me identify who exactly this

"Nah Me" is, a boy or a girl, big or small,

is this mischievous being short or tall?"

Silence filled the room. It was clear that

no one was willing to say who was

responsible for any of the many

mischiefs made.

"Hmmm!"

Mom let out a big sigh frustratingly, deciding to use this as a teaching opportunity.

As the five children sat looking at Mom attentively, she began,

"We are all guilty sometimes of doing something wrong, but when we are asked, it is best to take responsibility instead of blaming "Nah Me."

They all chuckled, as Mom smiled.

"When I was growing up "Nah Me" lived in our house too but my mother taught me just like I am teaching you the importance of telling the truth. I have heard each of you blame "Nah Me" for every mischief made, and it may seem easier to say but when you practise honesty, you will see, that sometimes, possibly most times, "Nah Me" just may be ...

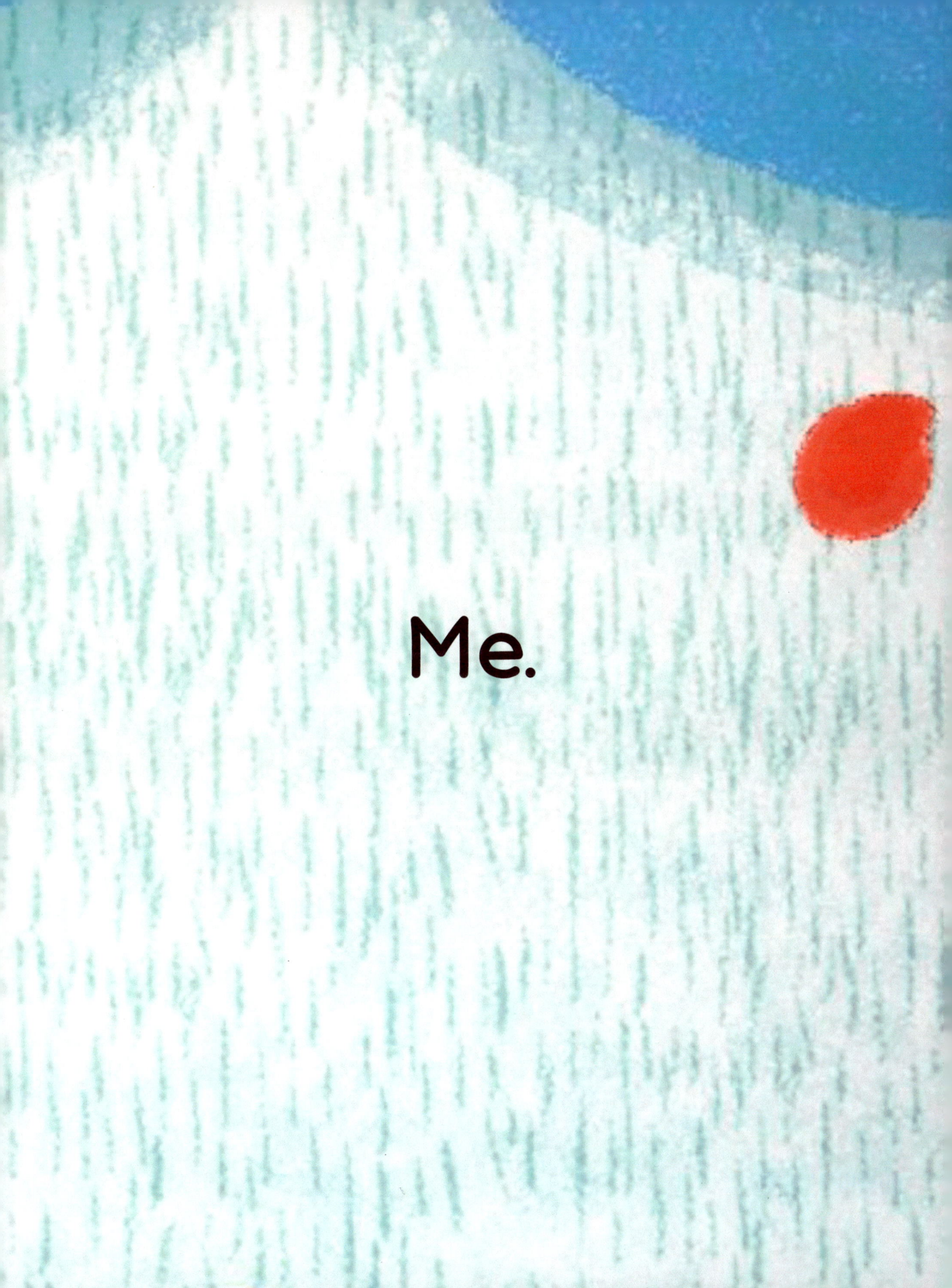

Me.

also by
Samantha Williams

I Am Me
Women! We All Can Rise: We All Can Shine!
I Am Me Too
A to Z Positive Affirmations for Boys and Girls
You Can, If You Try

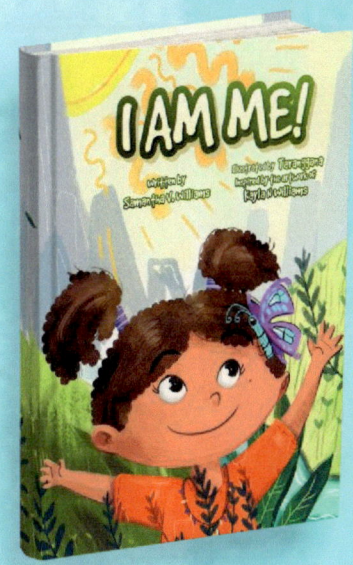
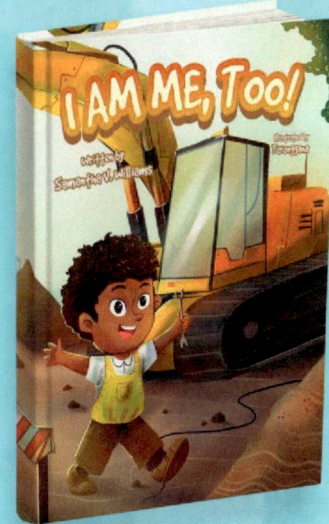
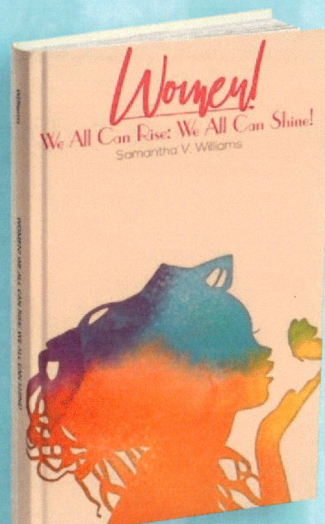
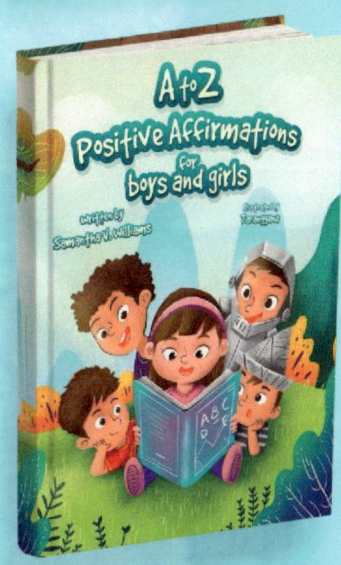
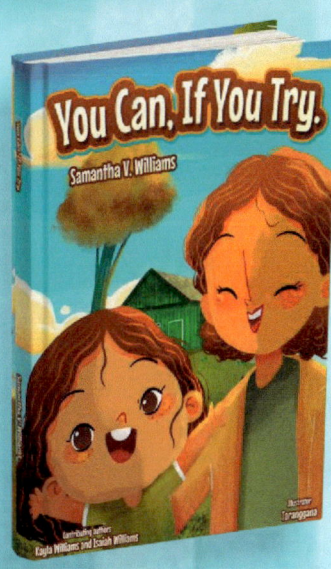

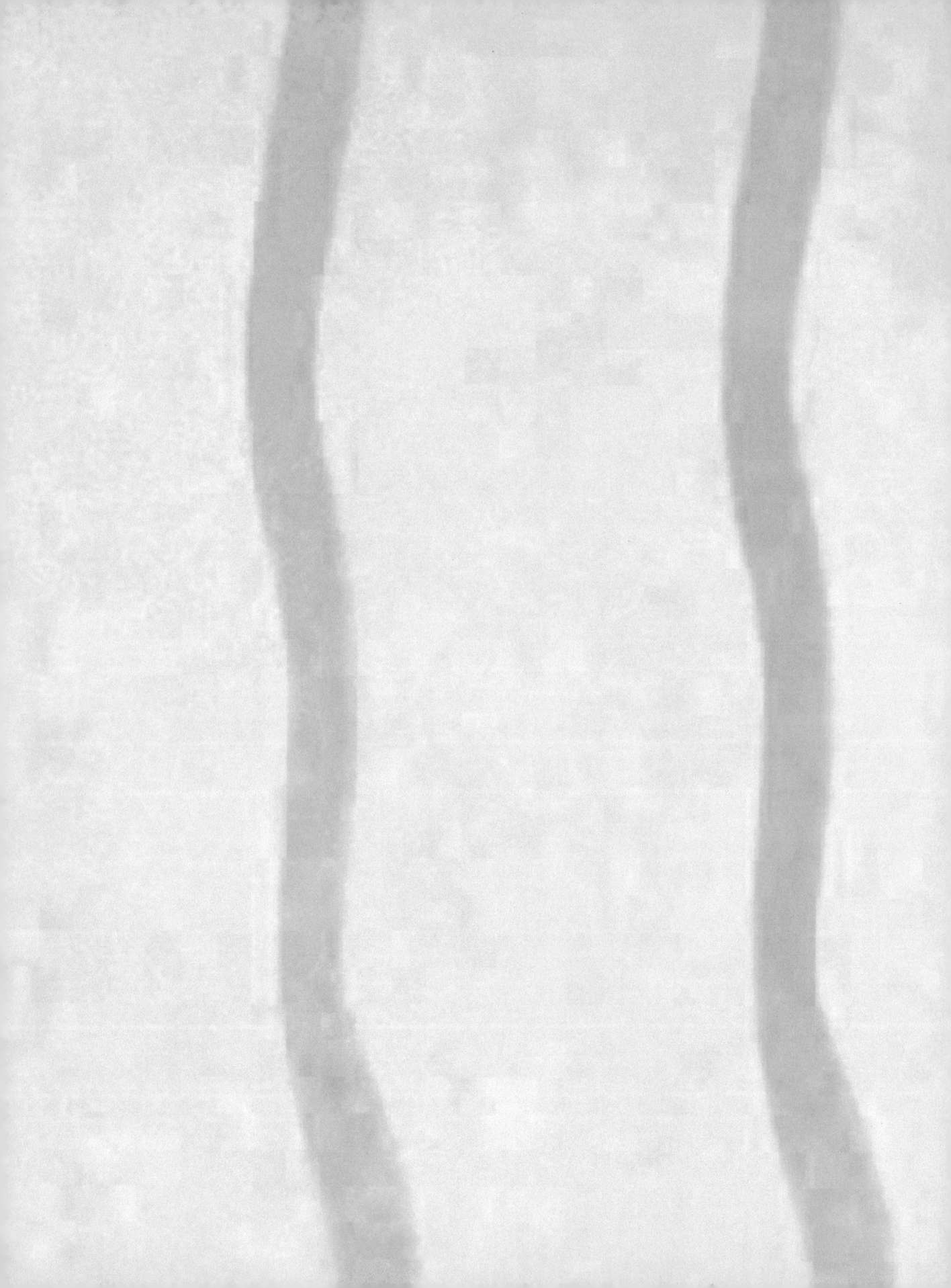

Made in the USA
Columbia, SC
05 January 2024

29947567R00015